BIG TOM

by Jean Ure

Illustrated by Chris Chapman

Collins

An imprint of HarperCollinsPublishers

For Ron, who was there; and Jan, who was also there but lived in Shirley.

First published in Great Britain in hardback by Collins in 2000
This edition published in paperback in 2000
Collins is an imprint of HarperCollins*Publishers* Ltd
77-85 Fulham Palace Road, Hammersmith, London W6 8JB

The HarperCollins website address is www.**fire**and**water**.com

5 7 9 8 6 4

Text copyright © Jean Ure 2000
Illustrations copyright © Chris Chapman 2000

ISBN 000 675153 9

The author and illustrator assert the moral right to be
identified as the author and illustrator of the work.

Printed and bound in Great Britain by
Omnia Books Limited, Glasgow

BIG TOM

Collins

RED

STORYBOOK

CHAPTER ONE

"Well," said Mum. "So that's it… it's happened!"

The Prime Minister, Mr Neville Chamberlain, had just made the announcement: Great Britain and Germany were at war.

Dad leaned forward and switched the wireless off. The clipped tones of the Prime Minister no longer filled the small sitting room. For a few minutes there was silence, as each member of the family thought about the announcement that had just been made.

Mum was thinking, "I hope Derek will be all right."

Derek was eighteen and had joined the army earlier that year. Would he be sent abroad to fight?

Dad was thinking, "Good job we got that shelter dug in."

The shelter was the Anderson, in the back garden. The Anderson would keep them safe when the bombs began to fall.

Elaine, who was sixteen, was thinking, "In a way, it's almost a relief."

The threat of war had been hanging over them for so long. Over the last few months, the talk had been of nothing else. Now, at least, they knew where they stood.

But Jenny, who was eleven, could only think of all the people and the animals that were going to be killed. She ran and buried her head in her mum's lap.

"There, there," said Mum, stroking her hair. "It'll all be over by Christmas."

Over? Bobbie was alarmed. How could Mum talk about it being over? It had hardly even begun! It couldn't be over by Christmas! Bobbie wanted it to go on until he was old enough to join the army, like his brother Derek. You couldn't join the army until you were eighteen. That meant the war had to go on for... Bobbie did some quick finger work. Nine years! *Could* a war go on that long?

"Dad," he said, "could the war go on for nine years?"

Elaine shrieked, "Don't! I'd be *ancient*!"

Jenny wailed, "Mum!" and clung with both arms round Mum's waist.

"It's all right, lovie. It's all right." Mum frowned, warningly, in Bobbie's direction. "Of course it won't go on for nine years. Nothing like. Hitler'll back down soon enough, don't you worry."

He'd better *not*, thought Bobbie. He looked pityingly at his sister. Everyone always said that Jenny was 'highly strung', meaning that she became easily upset. He supposed she couldn't help it. After all, she was only a girl. If girls had their way, there'd never be any fighting at all!

Bobbie ran to the window. He had a faint hope that the sky might already be full of German planes coming to drop their bombs. Not that they would be allowed to, of course. The ack-ack guns would blast them to smithereens, Boom, boom! Rat-a-tat-tat! In his mind, Bobbie could see them, wave upon wave, bursting into flames as they nose-dived to the ground. They might be nose-diving right now!

But the sky outside was clear and blue; not a plane in sight. You'd have thought they'd be here by this time!

Bobbie pressed his nose to the windowpane.

"When's it going to start?" he said, fretfully.

"Swelp me!" Dad laughed. "He can't wait, can he?"

"Seems to me," said Bobbie, "the sooner we get going the better."

"Bloodthirsty little beast," said Elaine.

"We're going to bomb the Germans!" Bobbie spread his arms and zoomed about the room being a bomber. A Wellington. Or maybe a Lancaster. He knew the names of all the planes. The German bombers were Heinkels, or Stukkas. Their fighter planes were Messerschmitts. Not a patch on the British Spitfire!

"Eeeeeeeeeaaaaaaaaaaa," droned Bobbie, zooming round the sofa.

"It's not a *game*," said Elaine. "You won't find it so funny when all the food's on ration and we're eating nothing but dry bread and potatoes every day."

"Don't care what I eat!" Bobbie zoomed off towards the door. "Eeeeeeeeee—"

He stopped. What was that? A ghostly wailing filled the air.

"It's the siren, it's the siren! It's begun!"

Jenny gave a little yelp.

"Right," said Dad. "You know the drill. Fetch your gas masks and out to the shelter. No need for panic! We've practised often enough."

Bobbie hoped his dad wasn't talking to *him*. He wasn't going to panic! He left that sort of thing to the girls.

But Elaine stayed calm and so did Jenny. Jenny had turned very pale, but she obediently picked up her gas mask in its cardboard case and went with Mum into the garden. The Anderson shelter had been dug right in the middle of Dad's lawn, Dad's beautiful velvety lawn that he had been so proud of. But he hadn't complained.

"Needs must," he'd said. "No sense grumbling." And he'd dug up the rest of the lawn as well, and planted vegetables – "for the war effort". Even the Anderson had vegetables growing on the top of it!

"Extra layer of earth," said Mum, and she patted Jenny's hand as they hurried down the path. "Makes it even safer."

Jenny gave a little shiver. Bobbie suddenly felt rather sorry for her. She might be two years older than him, but he had to remember she was just a girl.

"Don't worry, sis!" He gave her the thumbs-up. It

seemed a manly thing to do. "They won't be able to get at us down here."

Jenny smiled, a faint trembly smile. She was obviously trying very hard to be brave. It must be terrible, thought Bobbie, to be such a scaredy-cat. He jumped down into the shelter.

"It's going to be fun! Like camping out."

Elaine wrinkled her nose. "Pooh! It smells."

"Just damp," said Mum. "It's the earth."

"It's disgusting!"

"Better disgusting than dead," said a crotchety voice – old Miss Dunc – already down there. Miss Dunc lived next door. She didn't have room for a shelter because she was at the end of the terrace and her garden was just a tiny sliver, like a wedge of cheese. So Mum had said she could come and share with them.

"I lived through the First World War," she told Elaine. "You don't hear me complaining, do you?"

Elaine pulled a face. Miss Dunc was a real old crosspatch but Mum said you had to be good neighbours, especially in wartime.

It was quite cramped in the shelter with all five of them down there. Mum and Dad sat in deck chairs, Jenny, Bobbie and Elaine shared a camp bed, and Miss

Dunc had installed her own favourite armchair. The armchair took up far more than its fair share of space, but nobody dared to say anything.

"Maybe I'll think of building some bunk beds," muttered Dad.

"You're not getting me in a bunk bed," snapped Miss Dunc. "I'd sooner die sitting up, if it's all the same to you."

Jenny stared at her in anguish.

"Nobody's going to die." Dad said it very firmly. "Not in this shelter."

"Bombs couldn't get us down here," said Bobbie. He wanted to reassure his sister. Show her there was nothing to be afraid of. "Me and Dad, we dug it real deep. Didn't we?"

"We did," agreed Dad.

"*Real* deep. They'll just bounce off!"

They sat there in the shelter, clutching at their gas masks, waiting for – what? Nobody was quite sure. Not even Miss Dunc, who had lived through the First World War.

"That was a totally different sort of war," she said. And then she added, "Far worse than this."

Elaine rolled her eyes.

"Oh, you can laugh, miss! This is as nothing," said Miss Dunc.

She wouldn't say that when the bombs started to fall, thought Bobbie. But where were the bombs? Where were the planes? Where were the guns, blasting them from the skies?

"Nothing's happening." he said. "Shall I go and look?"

"No!" Mum grabbed hold of him. "Don't you dare to go outside!"

"But nothing's *happening*," said Bobbie.

And nothing did happen. Not that day. The all clear

went and they all trooped back outside and everything was just as they had left it.

"Must have been a false alarm," said Dad.

Everyone was relieved except Bobbie.

"What a swizz!" he said. "I thought it was supposed to have *started*."

CHAPTER TWO

"Bobbie Dobson!" said Mum. "You take your gas mask with you!"

"But we're only going to the sweet shop," said Bobbie.

The sweet shop wasn't even five minutes away. It was just three doors up, on the corner of Scarlet Street, where the Dobsons lived, and Station Road. What did Mum think was going to happen between here and the sweet shop?

"I don't care where you're going," said Mum. "You take that gas mask!"

Bobbie screwed his face into a hideous gargoyle expression. He tramped back into the hall and picked up the gas mask in its cardboard case. Jenny already had hers. Of course! Jenny always did what she was told. She never went anywhere without her gas mask.

"It's just stupid," grumbled Bobbie, as they walked down the path. "If the alarm went, we'd have bags of time to get back."

He meant if the alarm went for a gas attack. So far,

it hadn't happened. All Bobbie had ever used his gas mask for was frightening Jenny. He had put it on one night and crept into her bedroom making ghosty noises. It had been the best fun of the war!

"Stands to reason," he muttered. "Not going to hang around in the street, are we?"

"Doesn't make any difference," said Jenny. "You have to have it with you *at all times*."

Bobbie pulled another gargoyle face. Why was his sister such a goody-goody? Because she was a girl, he supposed.

"Nothing's going to happen," he said. "Nothing's ever going to happen."

The war was proving a great disappointment to Bobbie. It had been going on for months and life was hardly any different from how it had been before. Well, not in any *exciting* sort of way. Schools had closed for a short time, but they had very quickly opened again. Some children from the East End had been sent into the country, for fear of bombs, but then when there weren't any they had all been sent back.

Barrage balloons had gone up, and that had been quite interesting for a while. Bobbie had had high hopes of barrage balloons. But barrage balloons didn't actually *do* anything. They didn't fly around, they didn't have guns. They didn't even burst or blow up. All they did was just hang about in the sky.

The blackout had been fun too, just at first, before people had grown used to it. They had all gone blundering about in the pitch dark, walking into gateposts and stubbing their toes on the kerb and going "Ow!" and "Ouch!" and "What the blazes?" Dad had said the blackout was more of a menace than Hitler.

Certainly Hitler didn't seem to be doing very

much. Leastways, not in this country. Not as far as Bobbie could see. Not a single German airman had come parachuting out of the skies, not a single Messerschmitt had nose-dived into the back garden, not a single air raid had taken place. What was Hitler up to? He was either fighting a war or he wasn't!

Bobbie said this to his sister, and she looked at him reproachfully. "Anyone would think you *wanted* horrid things to happen!"

Not horrid things. Exciting things!

They reached the sweet shop and the bell tinkled as they opened the door. Mrs Beames sat behind the counter. Mrs Beames was like her name: she beamed. Mrs Beames was *always* beaming. She was plump and cosy like a big soft cushion and all the children loved her.

On top of the counter, in a warm fat heap, sat Big Tom. Big Tom was Mrs Beames's cat. He was rather like Mrs Beames: plump and soft and cosy. All the children loved him, too! Bobbie loved him best of all.

"Big Tom!" he cried, and he wrapped his arms round him and rubbed his cheek against Big Tom's fur. Big Tom purred loudly. He was an exceedingly handsome cat: glossy black, with four white socks, a white tip to his tail and white patches on his face.

Bobbie was his favourite of all the children who came into the shop.

"I wish Mum and Dad would let me have a cat," said Bobbie.

"Dear me! Then poor Tom would be so jealous," said Mrs Beames.

"Well, I'd still come and talk to him."

"Ah, but it wouldn't be the same. He'd know."

"Anyhow, you can't have one while the war's on,"

said Jenny. "It wouldn't be fair. What would it do if the Germans came and dropped bombs?"

"They're not going to drop bombs!" Bobbie sounded resentful. "They'd have done it by now if they were going to."

"I wouldn't be so sure about that," said Mrs Beames. "I reckon they're just biding their time. How's your Derek getting on?"

"Derek's in France." Jenny couldn't help a note of importance entering her voice. All the family were proud of Derek. "He's with the Expeditionary Force."

"Like my George."

But Mrs Beames's George was only a private. Derek had a stripe on his sleeve. He was a corporal! That was because Derek had volunteered; George had waited to be called up.

"Doing a good job out there, those lads." Mrs Beames nodded. "They'll have Jerry on the run in no time." When Mrs Beames said "Jerry", she meant the Germans.

Bobbie heaved a sigh. He scooped Big Tom into his arms and cradled him glumly.

"War'll be over before we've even had a chance."

"Well! And what are we supposed to make of that?" said Mrs Beames.

"He wants horrible things to happen." Jenny said it bitterly. "He wants bombs and air raids and planes shooting at each other."

"It's wartime!" roared Bobbie. "That's what happens in wartime!"

Mrs Beames shook her head. "I just hope you don't have your way, young man. Now, what can I do for you both?"

"Two ounces of Jelly Babies, please." Jenny opened her purse. "And the *Daily Mirror* for Mum."

"I'll have Liquorice Allsorts," said Bobbie.

"Please," prompted Jenny.

"Please. And two penn'orth of gobstoppers."

"Gobstoppers to stop your gabble." Mrs Beames reached for the jar. "Stop all that nasty talk of bombs and air raids."

"It won't happen, will it?" Jenny looked at Mrs Beames trustfully. "If we drive the Germans out of France—" She hesitated. "We will drive them out of France, won't we?"

"Lord love you, of course we will!" said Mrs Beames. "What with your Derek out there, and my George... them Jerries, they'll go running!"

"I told you so," said Bobbie, glumly, as they left the shop. "It'll all be over."

But Bobbie was wrong, and so was Mrs Beames. The Germans didn't go running; it was the British and their allies who had to run. Thousands of troops were evacuated from the beach at a place called Dunkirk that Bobbie had never heard of before. Fleets of boats – big boats, little boats, barges, dinghies, anything that would float – crossed the Channel to help in their rescue. Not everyone came home.

George Beames was one of the lucky ones. He made it back. He was wounded, but his wounds were not too serious. Mrs Beames went down to Kent to visit him in hospital, leaving Big Tom with Bobbie. Bobbie was enchanted.

"I do *wish* I had a cat of my own," he said.

"Bobbie, please don't start that again," said Mum. "This is not the time."

Bobbie was hurt. All he'd done was say that he wished he had a cat!

"You are just *so* insensitive," hissed Elaine. "All you ever think of is yourself! You know Mum's worried silly about Derek."

Derek was one of the ones who hadn't come back. No one knew where he was or what had happened to him.

"I forgot," mumbled Bobbie.

Elaine rolled her eyes. "You see? You see what I mean? You're such a selfish little toad!"

He didn't mean to be selfish but you couldn't worry *all* of the time. And Derek was bound to come home. George Beames had come home and he was only a private. Derek was probably still on his way. His boat had probably broken down or stopped in the wrong place. It had probably gone to Ireland or somewhere. He said this to Elaine and she looked at him with distaste, as if he were some kind of particularly repellent insect.

"Maybe you'll grow out of it," she said.

"Out of what?"

"Your present personality!" snarled Elaine.

Bobbie went to sit on top of the Anderson with Big Tom. There was something very strange about girls. They certainly weren't the same as boys.

In the House of Commons Mr Winston Churchill, who was now Prime Minister, made a stirring speech.

"We shall defend our island, whatever the cost may be. We shall fight on the beaches, we shall fight on the landing grounds. We shall fight in the fields and in the streets. We shall fight in the hills. We shall never surrender."

"Chin up, lovie!" said Mrs Beames, when she came to collect Big Tom. She put an arm round Mum's shoulders. "My George says there was so much confusion on that beach, no one hardly knew what was going on. Your Derek'll turn up safe and sound. You'll see!"

Mum smiled and tried to be brave, but the newspapers were full of scare stories.

GERMANY SET TO INVADE BRITAIN!

GERMAN INVASION IMMINENT

"What's imm'nent?" said Bobbie.

Jenny wasn't sure. "I think it means it could happen any day."

"Cor!"

Bobbie was impressed. An invasion! That was something he hadn't thought of.

Pictures appeared of railway stations with the names painted out and of beaches covered with barbed wire. Bobbie and his best friend Stanley Blackshaw dreamed of what they would do if they came across an invading German.

"What *would* you do?" said Elaine scornfully.

"We'd trail him!"

"And then what?"

"Then we'd corner him and go for the p'lice!"

"Huh!" said Elaine. "A likely tale!"

She was just scared, of course. It sometimes seemed to Bobbie that everyone was scared except him and Stanley Blackshaw. Well, and Dad. Nothing frightened Dad. But even Dad didn't have plans for catching German invaders.

In July the Battle of Britain began, the great struggle between the RAF and the German *Luftwaffe*. What Bobbie wouldn't have given to be a Spitfire pilot! He and Stanley Blackshaw watched the planes going over, wave upon wave of them. They even saw

the occasional dogfight up above them in the clouds. They played Battle of Britain games in the back garden, taking it in turns to be Spitfires and Messerschmitts. They looked for bits of shrapnel, and kept a watch for German pilots dangling at the end of parachutes.

"I suppose you're enjoying all this," said Elaine.

Bobbie regarded her sternly. "I'm not *enjoying* it. I'm *practising*."

"For what?"

"For when I find a German pilot!"

"Oh, for heaven's sake!" said Elaine. "Haven't you got anything better to do?"

It was all very well for Elaine. She had left school and was working. She was in a factory, making parts for aircraft. She was doing her bit for the war effort. Bobbie wasn't doing anything. Mum said he could help best by being good and behaving himself, but what use was that? He wanted to feel that he was part of things!

And then, at the beginning of September, they all became part of things. The siren sounded – Moaning Minnie, as people called it – and this time it was for real.

The bombs showered down upon London.

CHAPTER THREE

It was dark and dank in the Anderson shelter, but that didn't worry Bobbie. He thought it was a bit like camping out. He'd always wanted to camp out, him and Stanley Blackshaw in the back garden, in a tent. In some ways the Anderson was more fun than a tent. It was like a real little house, underground.

Miss Dunc took her teeth out – "In case we get a direct hit". She wrapped the teeth in a handkerchief and stowed them away in her big brown handbag. "I wouldn't want me teeth to go missing."

Bobbie knew from the look on Elaine's face that she disapproved of Miss Dunc taking her teeth out. Elaine was always very fastidious. She hated dirt and mess and anything that wasn't quite nice. Dad hadn't yet got around to making any bunk beds but Mum had put an old rag rug and a strip of lino on the ground so that if it rained they wouldn't have to sit with their feet in the mud. Even so, Elaine complained that it was disgusting.

"It stinks! It's revolting!"

"It's better than having to go down the Underground

28

like some poor folk," said Mum.

"Yeah." Bobbie's eyes gleamed. "There's rats down the Underground. Huge great ones, all crawling about." Stanley Blackshaw had told Bobbie about the rats. Stanley's family didn't have an Anderson. They'd be down there right now, down the Underground with the rats. "Whoppers, they are! Big as dogs. They run over people and bite 'em and—"

"Oh shut up!" said Elaine. "I wish I knew how long this air raid was going to go on. I haven't brought my curlers with me."

Elaine curled her hair up every night and went to bed festooned with pins, looking like a hedgehog. Did she sleep sitting up, or what? Bobbie would have given anything to know. But it wasn't the sort of thing you could ask her. She would only become tetchy.

"I like it down here," said Bobbie. "It's like a little house."

Elaine sniffed. "Not my idea of a house."

"We could have a little cupboard with some food. If we had food," said Bobbie, "we could stay here for days."

"Mum, can't you stop him?" wailed Elaine. "He's really getting on my nerves!"

Mum sighed. "He's only trying to make the best of things."

"He's not. He's enjoying it!"

"He wanted this to happen," said Jenny. "It's what he's been waiting for."

"He's bonkers," said Elaine.

"There's a *war* on!" roared Bobbie. "We're fighting a *war*!" You had to enter into the spirit of things. It wasn't any use moaning. "This is what happens in war!"

"Young man, will you please stop shouting?" said Miss Dunc. "We'll get more than enough noise before the night is out without you adding to it."

For quite a long time the only noise that anyone could hear was the noise of Miss Dunc herself, sleeping with her mouth open and snoring as she did so. Bobbie listened to the snores in fascination. He had never heard anything like them! The whole shelter shook as they rolled back and forth. Jenny started to giggle and had to clamp a hand over her mouth. Elaine just rolled her eyes. She was still fussing about her hair and wanting the air raid to be over so she could go back indoors and put her curlers in.

"Don't see how it can be *over*," said Bobbie,

"considering it's not yet hardly *begun*."

"I bet it's just another false alarm. I bet nothing's going to happen. I—"

Elaine never finished what she had been going to say. Before the words were properly out of her mouth, the world outside the shelter exploded. Jenny screamed and buried her head in Mum's lap. Miss Dunc woke up with a start.

"What is it? Have they got us? Have we been hit?"

"No! No. It's all right, Jenny love. It's not us."

"Some other poor soul," said Miss Dunc. (Except that she couldn't talk properly with her teeth out. Some was "thum" and soul was "thole".) "I wonder where it was?"

She cocked her head, birdlike, towards the roof of the shelter. As she did so, another explosion tore the night apart. Jenny screamed again, a piercing screech of terror, and Bobbie found that Elaine had both arms round him and was clutching him very tightly. Was she scared? Was *Elaine* scared? Bobbie wasn't. The shelter would save them. Dad had said so.

"Bombproof, that shelter."

Nobody could get them while they were in the Anderson. All the same, he did rather wish that Dad was with them. It would have been good to have another man there. But Dad was driving his train. King's Cross to Glasgow, his regular run, for the London Midland and Scottish Railway Company.

"That sounded rather too close for comfort," said Miss Dunc. "I reckon they must be right overhead. Know where they'll be making for, don't you?" She nodded wisely. "East End. The docks. That's where they'll be headed."

"So why are they dropping bombs on us?" shrieked Elaine.

"Got lost, most like. Don't know where they are. Th—"

Miss Dunc broke off. Elaine clasped Bobbie, Mum clasped Jenny. Somewhere outside there came a loud WHUMPF! They could hear the steady droning of the German bombers, and the rattle-tattle-tat of the British ack-ack guns, desperately trying to bring them down.

"That sounded like it was right in the garden!" gasped Elaine.

"It's OK, sis." Bobbie said earnestly. "They can't get

33

us so long as we're in the shelter."

"I know that!" snapped Elaine. "But we can't stay down here for ever!"

"I hope your dad's all right," said Mum. Train drivers couldn't go into shelters. All they could do was stop their trains, put out all the lights, and just sit tight and wait. Even Bobbie thought that that must be rather scary. He reckoned his dad was pretty brave, being a train driver.

"Glad I took me teeth out," said Miss Dunc. "Wouldn't want to lose me teeth."

At last the all clear sounded: the air raid was over. Miss Dunc put her teeth back in and they all trooped out of the shelter.

"Well! At least the house is still there," said Elaine.

The house *was* still there, and still in one piece; but all around was the smell of burning, and the jangling of bells as ambulances and fire engines raced through the streets.

"Fair bit of activity out there," said Miss Dunc. "Some poor devils must have copped it."

Miss Dunc went back to her own house. Elaine rushed upstairs to put her curlers in. "I'm going to look such a sight tomorrow!"

Lots of girls wore their curlers to work, hidden

under headscarves, but Elaine wouldn't do that. She was too proud.

"Suppose there was an air raid and I got killed? With my *curlers* in? I'd be so ashamed!"

Mum tucked Bobbie and Jenny into their beds. "Sleep tight," she said, "the planes have all gone now. You're safe."

Bobbie obediently closed his eyes but it took a long time to fall asleep. He was too keyed up. He had lived through an air raid! And he hadn't been scared. Now he couldn't wait for it to be daylight, so he could go outside and see what had happened.

Dad came home in time for breakfast. He was looking grave.

"Bad night," he said. "The East End got hammered. Good and proper."

Bobbie had only a vague idea where the East End actually was. Dad spoke of Poplar and Shoreditch, of Whitechapel and Stepney. But to Bobbie they were just names on the tube map. He had never been to any of them. He didn't know anyone who lived there.

"Mum," he said, "can I go out and play?"

"Yes, I suppose so," said Mum. "But be careful. Don't touch anything. And don't pick anything up!"

Bobbie was out of the house in a flash. He called in at Mrs Beames's, just to say hello.

"Some night, eh, Mrs Beames?"

"You can say that again, young fellow. I hear they caught it in the High Street."

Bobbie galloped off excitedly round the corner to Stanley Blackshaw's.

"Morning, Mrs Blackshaw!"

Mrs Blackshaw had her curlers in. She wasn't proud.

"Can Stan come out?"

"If he's got his eyes open," said Mrs Blackshaw. She turned and bellowed up the stairs. "*Stanley!* You awake? Someone for you." She turned back to Bobbie. "We bin down the Underground," she said. "Terrible, it was. All crowded. Everyone pushin' an' shovin'. Hardly got a wink. Oh, there you are." Stanley's face had appeared, somewhat blearily, at the top of the stairs. "If you're going out, you'd best take some bread an' dripping with you."

Stanley shared the bread and dripping with Bobbie as they set off down the road.

"Hear the High Street caught it," said Bobbie.

"Yeah?"

"Yeah."

There was a silence, as they munched on their bread and dripping.

"Mean it got bombed?" said Stanley.

"Yeah. Well – I guess so."

"Wanna go an' see?" said Stanley.

"Why not?"

The two of them went racing off. They reached the end of the road — and skidded to a halt. There, in the High Street, where once a row of shops had stood, was now a vast pile of rubble.

"Blimey!" said Stan.

Bobbie's eyes stood out on stalks. "What's that?"

"Where?"

"That, over there!"

Stanley looked where Bobbie was pointing. His jaw dropped open. His face turned muddy grey, the colour of putty.

"B-bodies?" He spoke in a whisper.

Together, the two boys crept forward. Bits of body lay scattered across the pavement. Arms and legs, heads and chests. Stanley stopped. His face was now a sickly yellow.

"Gonna chuck up!"

Bobbie felt his own stomach ballooning in sympathy. And then... he realized. He made a choking sound, halfway between a sob and a laugh.

"It's all right!" He dashed boldly ahead into the sea of bodies. "It's all right! Look!" He snatched up a leg and rushed at Stanley, whirling it above his head. Stanley stared at him as if he had gone mad. And then Stanley, too, suddenly realized. His face broke into a gap-toothed grin.

"Dummies!"

They were just the dummies from Lindsay Lee, the ladies' dress shop, which was now part of the pile of rubble.

"Cor!" said Stanley. "I thought for a minute it was people."

"Let's take a bit each for souvenirs!"

Bobbie had his leg, Stanley chose an arm. They stuffed them up the fronts of their jerseys and went scampering off, giggling guiltily.

"It's not like it's proper stealing," said Stanley. "I mean… they're all broke."

"Yeah." Bobbie tightened his hold on the leg, bulging out of the front of his jersey. "All messed up. Couldn't be used again."

Bobbie arrived home and went marching triumphantly up the garden path. It was Mum who let him in.

"What have you got there?" she said, looking suspiciously at the bulge in his jumper.

"Something I found."

"What? Where did you get it from?"

"Found it in the High Street."

"So what is it?"

"It's a leg," Bobbie said solemnly.

"A *leg*?" Jenny had come into the hall. Her eyes whizzed round like saucers.

"Off of a dead person. Wanna see?"

"*No!*" Jenny and Mum both yelled it at the same time, but too late. Bobbie had already pulled out his trophy and was holding it aloft.

Jenny fainted. And Mum was furious. So was Dad. "Things like that, son, are just not funny."

Bobbie couldn't understand it. Did *no one* have a sense of humour in his family?

CHAPTER FOUR

Now the war was starting to be a bit more like a war. A bit more as Bobbie had imagined a war would be. The German planes came over regular as clockwork, droning in from the Kent coast on their way to bomb the East End. Every night, Bobbie and his family huddled in the Anderson, waiting for the all clear to sound so that they could go back to their beds and try to snatch a bit of sleep before it was time to get up again for work or for school.

Miss Dunc was the only person who ever managed to sleep in the shelter. She took out her teeth and wrapped them in her handkerchief and settled down for her nightly snore. Elaine complained bitterly to Mum.

"How can we get any rest with that racket going on? She drives me crazy! Why can't she go down the Underground like everyone else?"

Mum was quite snappish.

"I'll thank you to remember she's an old lady! Just try to show a bit more charity."

Mum wasn't normally a snappy kind of person, but

she had a lot to cope with. She worried about Dad when he was driving his train; she worried about Derek, posted missing after Dunkirk; she worried about Jenny, who still screamed and buried her head every time a bomb exploded. She worried about how to 'make do' and whether the family was getting enough to eat. She stood in queues for hours on end at the butcher's and the baker's and the greengrocer's. She didn't need Elaine's grumbles.

"I know it's hard on you young folk," she said, "the best years of your life and having to spend them like this. But it's even harder on the old ones. They haven't got the same resources. So you just be quiet and learn to put up with things, my girl! Try taking a leaf out of your brother's book. You don't hear him moaning and groaning all the time."

Elaine tossed her head and said that Bobbie didn't have anything to moan and groan about.

"He's having the time of his life!"

It was true that Bobbie was quite enjoying himself.

"I'm making the best of things," he said.

"No, you're not. You're wallowing in it. You're like a ghoul! You don't care that people are getting killed. You don't care they're getting bombed out of their homes. You don't *care* they have to go round like scarecrows because they haven't any decent clothes to wear. Haven't even got any *stockings*. I am just so FED UP!" cried Elaine.

She went dashing from the room. There was a silence. Dad put down his newspaper.

"Should I go and talk to her?"

"No." Mum said it wearily. "Leave her. She'll get over it. It's just a phase she's going through."

By the next day Elaine was back to her old self again. Doreen Jackson, her best friend at work, had given her some brown stuff in a bottle that she could paint her legs with so that it looked as though she was wearing stockings.

"See?" She came prancing into the kitchen and did a little twirl. "You'd never know the difference!"

She had even painted lines down the backs of her legs in a darker shade of brown to make it look like the stockings had seams.

"What happens if it rains?" said Bobbie, with interest.

"What do you mean, what happens if it rains?"

"Does it wash off?"

"Of course it doesn't wash off, stupid! It's a *dye*."

"I told you she'd get over it," said Mum.

Now that she could walk around with painted

legs, Elaine was happy. She had even stopped grumbling about Miss Dunc and her snoring. She rolled her eyes and pursed her lips and heaved big dramatic sighs, but she didn't actually say anything.

This was just as well as Mum had her hands full looking after Jenny. Just lately, when the bombs fell, Jenny hadn't screamed or buried her head in Mum's lap; instead, she had sat bolt upright, still as a statue,

her teeth clenched and her hands balled into two tight fists. If you touched her, she felt cold and stiff; if you talked to her, she didn't reply. Even her eyes didn't move. She was locked into her own icy world of terror.

"You know Mrs Parker's dog Bonzo?" said Bobbie. "Mrs Parker stuffs cotton wool in his ears so he doesn't get frightened."

"Mrs Parker's dog should have been sent to the country," said Mum. "It's not fair on animals, keeping them in town."

"No, but what if we stuffed cotton wool in Jenny's ears?"

Mum was frowning. "It might be better if we sent Jen into the country."

But Jenny burst into a passion of tears when Mum suggested it.

"I don't want to leave you! Please, Mum! Don't make me leave you!"

Bobbie felt sorry for Jenny, though he did think she should have realized by now that the Anderson was quite safe. He had told her often enough.

"They can't get us down here."

By the time the bombers had passed over, Jenny had worked herself into such a state that she needed to go to the toilet. Miss Dunc always brought a big china potty with her – "In case I get caught short" – but Jenny wouldn't use it. She was too shy. Mum said, "No one will see you. I'll hold my coat over you." But Jenny whispered, "They'd hear me!"

Bobbie told Stanley Blackshaw about it as they roamed the streets together, looking for shrapnel.

"You got to understand," said Stanley, "girls is *diff'rent* from us."

"Glad I'm not a girl," said Bobbie.

Girls didn't have any fun at all! For Bobbie and Stanley, the streets were like a big adventure playground. There were bomb sites to be explored, piles of rubble to be clambered over, burnt-out houses to be investigated. Jenny would never go with them. She said it was dangerous.

"Mum's told you over and over not to do that sort of thing!"

Jenny just played skipping games and hopscotch with her friends. But you could play skipping games and hopscotch at any time! They had been playing those games before the war. Girls just didn't seem to enjoy themselves they way boys did.

"Some people," said Elaine, "happen to be a little bit more sensitive than others. Some people don't *want* to run the risk of breaking their necks or getting blown up by unexploded bombs."

Unexploded bombs! Oh boy! Wouldn't that be something?

"Reckon we might find any?" said Bobbie casually to Stanley.

"Might do," said Stanley. The idea rather thrilled them.

"Not got to touch 'em," urged Bobbie.

"Nah! Call the p'lice."

"Might get a medal!"

After that, they spent much of their spare time searching for bombs. Neither of them was quite sure what a bomb looked like, which made it rather difficult. Bobbie thought they might be "little round things with spikes", while Stanley had a notion they were "long and sausage-shaped".

One day, clambering about a ruined house, they stumbled upon something which looked as if it could be one. It wasn't little or round, and it wasn't exactly long and sausage-shaped. But it did look awfully bomblike.

The two boys stood dead still, not daring to move, hardly even daring to breathe.

"What d'you reckon?" whispered Bobbie.

"Dunno." Stanley licked his lips. "Could be. On the hand—"

Bobbie waited. On the other hand...

"What?"

"Could just be an old petrol tank."

"You reckon?"

"Well... could be."

The petrol tank (or bomb) was just two feet away from them, lying in a ditch where Bobbie had kicked it. He hadn't meant to kick it.

"My foot just sort of... touched it 'fore I knew it was there."

Which was, of course, exactly the way it happened with unexploded bombs.

"What'll we do?"

They couldn't just stand there waiting for it to explode.

"Count of five," said Stanley. "Make a run for it. One... two... "

He had reached as far as four when from somewhere above them there came a grinding, splintering sound as the roof beams collapsed and a shower of slates and timber came thundering down. Bobbie and Stanley hurled themselves to the ground and covered their heads with their arms. Slates bounced

off the bomb (or petrol tank) and went rolling away into the ditch. The two boys held their breath. It was a nasty moment.

When at last they dared to look up again, the bomb (or petrol tank) was still there – a little bit dented, a little bit battered, but otherwise in one piece. Surely, if it had been a bomb, it would have gone off?

"Told you," said Stanley, though he sounded a little shaky. "It's a petrol tank."

They waited. Nothing happened.

"Told you," said Stanley again. He sounded a little bolder this time. Slowly he began to inch forward, keeping low to the ground. "Yeah! Look. There's its badge."

Bobbie raised his head. He could just make out the letters BSA.

"A Beezer!" Stanley scrambled to his feet. "My uncle's got one."

Bobbie breathed a sigh of relief. He didn't reckon his mum would have been too pleased if a policeman had come knocking at the door to tell her that her younger son had been blown up. Not with the older one posted missing.

"*Could* have been a bomb," said Stanley. "Could have been a dud. You get 'em from time to time."

"What's this stuff?"

Bobbie had picked up a chunk of metal that had fallen off the roof.

"That's lead, that is." Stanley knew about such things. Before the war, his dad had been a builder. "Bluey."

"Bluey?"

"It's what it's called."

"Bluey." Bobbie weighed it in his hand. "Strike me

pink!" he said, imitating his dad. "Weighs a ton!"

"It's valuable, that stuff." Stanley bent down and heaved up a large lump. "Take it round to old Grimes, he'd give us money for it."

"You reckon?"

"Yeah! It's in demand, innit? Scrap metal."

"How much you reckon he'd give us?"

"Dunno. Bob or two."

"Let's take it!"

The lead was so heavy they could only carry a small amount. Even so, old Grimes gave them sixpence each.

"Sixpence," marvelled Stanley. "That's more'n I get pocket money!"

"We could go back and get more," urged Bobbie.

"Need something to carry it in."

"I know! We could take my sister's dolls' pram."

Jenny didn't use her dolls' pram any more, but it was still there in the outhouse. Nobody would know if Bobbie just borrowed it.

Next day was Sunday. Stanley and Bobbie – the Bluey Men – collected three loads of lead in their dolls' pram and trundled it down to old Grimes.

"Well done, lads." Old Grimes was pleased with them. "I reckon that's worth two-and-a-tanner."

Two-and-a-tanner. Bobbie gulped. Two-and-sixpence. Half-a-crown! They were rich!

After that they stopped looking for unexploded bombs and started looking for lead. The Bluey Men were in business!

Elaine saw them one day, wheeling their dolls' pram up the road.

"What *are* you doing?" she said. "Playing at daddies?"

"We're helping the war effort," said Bobbie, importantly.

On their fifth trip to old Grimes, a policeman was waiting for them.

"Now then, you kids," he said. "I've had my eye on you."

Bobbie and Stanley were marched home in disgrace.

"How was I to know?" wailed Bobbie. "I didn't know it *belonged* to anyone."

"Well, Bobbie, of course it does," said Mum. "It belongs to the people who lived in the houses. And I've told you before," she added, "that you are *not* to go clambering about on bomb sites!"

"I was only trying to help the war effort," muttered Bobbie.

"Well, you won't help it by disobeying my orders and by helping yourself to other people's property. You get up to your bedroom and you stay there. I'm very disappointed in you."

It was terrible, thought Bobbie, to be so misunderstood. He clumped up the stairs, clutching Big Tom in his arms. Big Tom often came to pay them a visit.

"Come to see me, don't you?" crooned Bobbie.

He and Big Tom curled up together under the eiderdown. Big Tom purred loudly. He didn't find Bobbie a disappointment. Bobbie was his favourite person.

"I don't know what I'd do without you," whispered Bobbie. "You're the only one who loves me."

CHAPTER FIVE

The war was really hotting up. One day the siren went while Bobbie was at school. Miss Gates, his teacher, immediately clapped her hands and cried, "Right, everyone. You all know what to do. Put on your gas masks and get beneath your desks."

Stanley scuttled across the room and came to join Bobbie under his desk. They crouched there together, screwing up their noses at each other inside their gas masks, trying to wobble the snouts and make piggy faces.

Some of the girls were scared. Maybe some of the boys were too. Albert Dredge and Billy Bosworth – a right couple of cowardy-custards! Bobbie had once chased Albert halfway across the playground with a dead mouse. As for Billy Bosworth, he burst into tears if he just scraped a finger. Bad as girls, those two. Bobbie and Stanley weren't scared! They had already looked death in the face with the unexploded bomb. Well, all right, the unexploded petrol tank. But it could have been a bomb. They weren't to know.

The air raid didn't last very long. Bobbie thought it was rather a pity. If it had gone on all morning they might have missed the spelling test Miss Gates had threatened them with. Bobbie wasn't too good at spelling. He would sooner have an air raid than a spelling test any day of the week.

They all crawled out from under their desks and put their gas masks back in their cardboard boxes.

"Hands up anyone who needs to go to the toilet?"

said Miss Gates.

A whole forest of hands went shooting up. But not Bobbie's. Not Stanley's. They would have scorned to go rushing to the toilet just because of a little thing like an air raid! They watched, pityingly, as Albert and Billy joined the long trail out of the classroom.

"All right, you two." Miss Gates turned to them with a happy beam. "Maybe you'd like to hand out the papers for the spelling test?"

That evening, there was another air raid. They were all so used to them by now that they were down in the shelter almost before Moaning Minnie had stopped her moaning.

"I hate that siren," said Elaine. "I'd like to strangle it!"

The shelter was becoming quite homely. They always carried their pillows and blankets with them, and Mum would bring a Thermos flask full of hot sweet tea and maybe a packet of biscuits. They all brought torches as well, so that they could read or play games. Jenny had her Enid Blyton books, Bobbie had his comics, Elaine had her magazines. Mum and Dad had the *Daily Mirror* or the *News of the World*. Miss Dunc went to sleep and snored. They hardly noticed her snoring these days. Even Elaine had stopped rolling her eyes. And not even Jenny screamed any more when the German planes came roaring overhead. She seemed to have accepted, at last, that down in the Anderson they were safe.

Only Elaine still turned up her nose and complained that it smelt. A girl at work, she said, had an *indoor* shelter.

"A Morrison. It's lovely. It's like a big cage. They keep it in the front room."

"I'm not sure I'd like a big cage in my front room," said Mum.

"But, Mum, it's *clean*. And it's dry. And it doesn't *smell*."

"Bet it's not as good as the Anderson," said Bobbie. He felt very loyal towards the Anderson. After all, he had helped Dad dig it in.

That night the air raid went on for longer than usual. It was four o'clock in the morning before the all clear sounded and they were able to go back indoors. Jenny, by that time, was bursting to use the toilet.

"Off you go," said Mum. "Then straight to bed."

Jenny went hurtling up the stairs. Seconds later, she gave a loud screech.

"*Mu-u-uum!*"

"What?" Mum was up there in a trice, quickly followed by Dad.

"Mum, there's smoke. The house is on fire!"

"Blimey!"

Bobbie made an excited dash for the stairs, only to be thrust out of the way by Dad galloping back down.

"Quick! We've got an incendiary bomb. We need water. Get the stirrup pump!"

Dad and Elaine raced to the kitchen and began filling buckets at the sink. Bobbie grabbed the stirrup pump. They all flew back upstairs.

Clouds of smoke were billowing from Mum and Dad's bedroom. Mum and Jenny were on the landing with wet towels clamped to their mouths. Dad seized the pump from Bobbie.

"Bobbie, you stay there! Elaine, come with me."

Elaine hurried after Dad into the bedroom. So did Bobbie. He wasn't going to be left out!

Dad dipped the pump into one of the buckets, sucked up the water, aimed the pump at the ceiling and squirted. Dip, suck, squirt. Dip, suck, squirt.

"More water!" shrieked Elaine.

Bobbie snatched up the empty bucket and ran with it to the door. Mum took it from him, filled it

from the bathroom tap and hurried back.

Dip, suck, squirt. Dip, suck, squirt.

It took six full buckets before the fire was put out. The bedroom and everything in it was sodden. Part of the ceiling had come down and the whole room smelt of smoke. The whole *house* smelt of smoke. Dad and Elaine were dripping wet. Everyone was choking.

They spent the rest of the night in the Anderson. Mum and Dad slept in the deck chairs, Elaine curled up in Miss Dunc's armchair, Jenny and Bobbie shared the camp bed. Even when they went indoors in the morning, the house still reeked of smoke. Fortunately the weather was dry and warm for the time of year, so Mum said she would open all the windows and doors and let the place air.

"But I'm blessed if I know what we're going to do about the bedroom," she sighed.

On their way to school, Jenny and Bobbie called in on Mrs Beames. Bobbie was full of the incendiary bomb and how he and Dad — well, and Elaine — had put it out.

"Whoosh!" He squirted an imaginary pump at Mrs Beames's ceiling. Big Tom watched with interest. "Whoosh! Water everywhere!"

"Oh, your poor mum!" said Mrs Beames. "What a mess!"

"Up in the roof, it was. Could have set the whole house alight."

"I was the one that found it," said Jenny, anxious to take some of the credit. "I went up to the toilet and there was all smoke coming out of the bedroom."

"Dearie me." Mrs Beames clicked her tongue. "Still, it could have been worse. That's one way of looking at it. Any news yet of your Derek?"

Jenny shook her head sadly. "They just say he's missing."

"He'll turn up, lovie. Don't you worry."

Round the corner in Bynes Road there was a house without any front. The whole of the wall had been ripped out so that you could see right inside.

"Cor! Look at that," breathed Bobbie. "You can see the stairs and everything!"

"Don't. It's horrid." Jenny tugged at his sleeve. "Stop gawping!"

But Bobbie couldn't help it. He was fascinated. You could even see inside the bathroom.

"Imagine if someone had been sitting on the toilet!"

"*Bob-bee!*" Jenny was shocked. "Don't be so disgusting!"

Bobbie could have gone on looking at the house all day, but Jenny wouldn't let him. She dragged him away saying they would be late for school. As if Bobbie cared. Lots of the kids arrived late these days. All you had to say was "Please, miss, the road was blocked," or "Sorry, miss, I couldn't get through." The teachers couldn't check on everyone. After all, there was a war on.

In Mapley Street they met a boy called Philip Spode. Philip was fourteen and went to the big school. They wouldn't normally have spoken to him, but Bobbie couldn't resist the temptation to do a bit of boasting.

"Hey! Guess what?" he crowed.

"What?" said Philip.

"Had an incendiary bomb, didn't we? Landed on the roof. Didn't half burn! Me and Dad," Bobbie swaggered, "we used the pump on it."

"Whizzo," said Philip.

Bobbie swaggered a bit more.

"Are you going to tell *everyone?*" said Jenny.

Well, why shouldn't he? He'd helped Dad save the house!

They walked on, up Mapley Street and into Badgers Green Road. School was at the far end.

"There's Miss Gates," said Bobbie. He waved at her. "We had an incendiary bomb last night, miss!"

"Dear me," said Miss Gates. "I hope it didn't do too much damage?"

"No. Me and Dad put it out," said Bobbie.

"Thank goodness for that!"

"You are perfectly *hateful*," said Jenny, as Miss Gates went on her way.

Bobbie looked at her, puzzled. Now what had he done?

"Going round blowing your own trumpet like that! What about poor Mum and her bedroom?"

Bobbie frowned. "Bedroom'll be all right. It only got a bit wet."

"It won't be all right! It's *ruined*. It's very upsetting for her. She and Dad worked really hard to get nice things for the house."

"It's only furniture," mumbled Bobbie. "Not like anyone got killed."

"Derek might have been." Tears spurted into Jenny's eyes. "Mum's already worried sick about him, and now this. And you just go round boasting about it!"

Bobbie felt a twinge of conscience. He hadn't thought too much about Derek just lately. It was true that people did get killed. Albert Dredge's brother had been. And Stanley had a cousin that was a pilot and had been shot down, only he'd been taken prisoner.

Bobbie cheered up slightly. Maybe that's what had happened to Derek?

"I bet he's been taken prisoner. I bet that's what it is. Prisoner in a prison camp. Be OK there," said Bobbie. "Safest place of all, in a prison camp."

"Are you completely *loopy*?" screeched Jenny. "People can *die* in prison camps!"

"Yeah, an' they can escape an' all," said Bobbie. "That's what I'd do if I was in a prison camp. I'd dig a tunnel and I'd escape!"

"Yes, and then you'd probably be *shot*," said Jenny.

It crossed Bobbie's mind that Jenny was a bit of a defeatist.

"I bet if you was old enough, you'd be a conchie!" he said.

Conchies were people that wouldn't go and fight. Jenny drew herself up, very stiff and straight.

"You have no right to say that!"

"You'd be too scared!" jeered Bobbie.

The tears spurted back into Jenny's eyes. "You are just so *hateful* at times!"

He did feel rather mean. But Jenny had a most annoying habit of ruining all his fun. Suppose Derek really had been killed? I'm not going to think about it, thought Bobbie; and he went running off across the playground.

"Hey, Stan! We had an incendiary bomb!"

When they arrived home from school that afternoon, Mum met them at the door with a big smile on her face.

There, thought Bobbie. She doesn't mind a scrap about her bedroom.

It was a bit odd, all the same. Mum wasn't house-proud, but she did like things to look nice.

"Wonderful news!" Mum waved a slip of paper at them. "Derek's alive and well!"

"Oh, *Mum!*" Jenny tossed her satchel into the air. Mum was laughing and crying, both at the same time. Bobbie poked his sister in the ribs.

"What did I tell you?" he said. "I told you he'd be OK."

He stomped through into the hall. All this fuss they made. He'd known all along there was nothing to worry about.

CHAPTER SIX

Bobbie and Stanley were out with the dolls' pram again, only this time it was Jenny who was pushing it. Jenny, and her friend Joan, whose sister Doreen had given Elaine the brown stuff for her legs. The four of them were looking for scrap. Old saucepans, old tin cans, old coat hangers, bits and pieces of broken toys, anything that could be recycled and used to help the war effort. When they had a pramful, they would take it to old Grimes.

"And the money is going to war orphans," Jenny reminded Bobbie. "It's not *our* money. We're doing it for *them*."

"I know, I know." Bobbie said it impatiently. Jenny did keep on so.

Along the side of the pram, in big letters, they had painted the words: COLLECT SCRAP. HELP THE WAR EFFORT.

"See?" Jenny pointed to it. She looked at Bobbie sternly. Mum had told her all about the exploits of the Bluey Men.

"We been into all this already," said Stanley.

"Yeah? Well, we'll all go down old Grimes's together," said Joan. It was plain *she* didn't trust them either. She probably didn't trust any boys. Girls were like that. Always seemed to think you were up to no good.

"Know what they said, 'bout the war being over by Christmas?" said Stanley. "My nan reckons that's a load of old cobblers."

"What's cobblers?" said Jenny.

"Load of old rubbish. She reckons it'll still be going this time next year."

"I heard someone say it'll still be going in ten

years' time," volunteered Joan.

"Ten years? Blimey!" Bobbie swung round, excited. "We'd be old enough to join up!"

"Goes on that long," said Stanley, "they might let us join sooner."

"Might let us join at fifteen."

"Might let us join at *fourteen*."

"Might not let you join at all," said Joan.

"That's right," said Jenny. She always agreed with Joan. "Who wants boys?"

Bobbie's face turned scarlet. "Be a sight more use than all them women they got!"

Bobbie was secretly disapproving of women being allowed to join the forces. Women weren't any good. They couldn't fight.

"Boy soldiers," he said. "That's what they ought to have."

Jenny gave a crow of laughter. Joan made a rude raspberry noise. Bobbie turned his back on them.

"Which lot'd you join?" he said to Stanley. "Navy, I s'pose, 'cos of your dad."

Stanley's dad was on the HMS *Belfast*. The *Belfast* was a battleship, but Stanley said *he'd* like to be on a submarine.

"Of course," Joan nodded kindly. "That would be

the safest, probably, wouldn't it?"

"*Safest?*" spluttered Stanley.

"Well, under the water."

"Where they couldn't get at you," said Jenny.

The two boys stared at them.

"Are you stupid, or what?" said Bobbie.

"You mind your manners," said Jenny. Joan ran at him with the pram.

"Gerroff!" shrieked Bobbie.

"Well, you just keep a civil tongue in your head. Me an' Jen ain't interested in that sort of thing. Are we?" said Joan.

"No, we're not," said Jenny. "*Boys.*" Her tone was scornful. "All they ever want to do is fight."

"There's a *war* on!" roared Bobbie. Fighting was what happened in a war. It was what it was all about. "You got to fight or you'll lose the war!"

"Oh shut up!" said Joan.

They were halfway down Bynes Road when Moaning Minnie started up. They stopped, shocked. It was the first time they had ever been out by themselves at the start of an air raid. Bobbie and Jenny had once been caught in the High Street, but that had been with Mum, doing the shopping. They had all dived down the nearest shelter and stayed there until it was over.

Maybe that was what they should do now? They stood, uncertain. A man pedalled past on a bicycle. He waved at them angrily.

"Get off the street, you kids!"

"Quick!" Jenny swung the pram round. "Let's go home!"

She and Joan started running, pushing the pram between them. After a moment's hesitation, the two boys followed. Bump bumpity bump, went the pram over the broken paving stones. The girls' legs were moving so fast they looked like the legs of cartoon characters. Even though they were boys, Bobbie and Stanley found it hard to keep up.

"Come on!" shrieked Jenny. There was panic in her voice. "We got to get back!"

Bobbie redoubled his efforts. Was he imagining it, or could he really hear the familiar drone of the German Heinkels coming over to drop their bombs? He risked a quick glance up at the sky. It was heavy and overcast and he could see nothing but the ghostly shape of a barrage balloon, hanging like a great white whale amongst the clouds. But he could definitely hear the roar of aeroplane engines somewhere overhead.

"*Bob-bee!*" Jenny broke away from the pram and grabbed him by the hand. Bobbie stumbled and nearly fell. He was smaller than she was, that was the

trouble. Let him grow just one more inch and he'd beat her hollow!

Joan reached her house and flew up the path with the pram.

"You can come in our shelter if you like!" she screeched over her shoulder at Stanley. Everyone knew the Blackshaws didn't have a shelter of their own. Stanley, with an apologetic glance at Bobbie, shot after Joan like a rabbit down its hole.

"See you later!"

"Yeah." Bobbie just managed to flap a hand before Jenny dragged him with her round the corner.

"Hurry!"

They found Mum dithering at the kitchen door.

"There you are. Thank goodness! Quick, quick, into the shelter!"

As they raced down the garden Bobbie took one last look up at the sky. Great black shapes were pouring out of the clouds. Heinkels! He almost fell into the shelter, tugged there by Mum.

"Heinkels!" He pointed. "Dozens of 'em!"

"Where are Stanley and Joan?" said Mum.

"Gone into Joan's. Mum, he's up there! Jerry's up there!"

A sudden furious burst from the ack-ack guns

drowned out Bobbie's voice. From somewhere there came the sound of an explosion.

"Oh, my Lord!" said Miss Dunc. "They're getting a bit bold, aren't they? Eleven o'clock in the morning?" She fumbled with her handkerchief. "Where's me teeth gone? What have I done with me teeth? Gawd! I hope I ain't dropped 'em!"

"Bobbie, have a look for Miss Dunc's teeth," said Mum.

"Yeah, and you just be careful you don't put your great feet on 'em!"

Bobbie obediently dropped to all fours and began crawling about the floor of the shelter.

"Do you mind?" said Elaine crossly. "That's my foot you're groping."

He didn't know what Elaine was doing there anyway. Why wasn't she at work, helping the war effort?

"I am not at *work*," said Elaine, "because I am starting on *nights*. I had hoped," she added bitterly, "to get in a bit of rest."

They were all there except Dad, who was driving his train.

"You got those teeth yet?" said Miss Dunc.

The teeth were found in the potty, which fortunately, was empty.

"Might as well put 'em back in me mouth," said Miss Dunc. Elaine shuddered. Miss Dunc looked at her sharply. "What's your problem, miss? You wait till you get to my age and lose your teeth. Won't find it quite so funny then."

"Don't find it funny now," muttered Elaine.

The air raid went on and on. Bobbie began to grow bored. He had long since read all his comics.

What else was there? He tried looking at Jenny's Enid Blytons, but they were all girls' stuff —*Twins at St Clare's*, *Naughtiest Girl in the School*. He didn't want to read about *girls*.

"Do you have to keep fidgeting?" said Elaine. "That's twice you've kicked me."

"I can't help it," said Bobbie. "I'm bored."

"You mean your legs just kick out, all by themselves?"

"Please, you two," begged Mum. "Don't make things worse than they have to be."

"Well, he's such a pain." Elaine drew her legs up and tucked them beneath her.

"What would you do," Bobbie leaned forward, "if you went outside and found a German pilot hanging in the apple tree?"

"Leave him there," snapped Elaine.

"*Seriously.*"

"I know what I'd do," said Mum. "I'd go down the road and tell Mr Gooch."

Mr Gooch was their local ARP warden. He was the man who made sure that people went into the shelters and had no lights showing from their windows.

"Dunno what good he'd be," said Bobbie.

"Well, what good would you be?" said Elaine.

"Better than you! I'd get my water pistol and threaten to shoot him. He wouldn't know it was a water pistol."

Elaine made a scoffing noise and went back to her magazine. Bobbie switched his torch on and off a few times. Dot-dot. Dash-dot.

"I know how to say hands up in German," he announced. "Stanley's uncle told him. It's hendy hock. Well, something like that."

"Why are you wasting that torch battery?" said Mum.

"I'm practising Morse code." Dot-dot, dash-dash-dot. "If I was on the beach and I saw a German U-boat making signals, I'd be able to send him false ones and lure him onto the rocks. Like this!" Bobbie pointed the torch at Elaine. Dot-dot-dash, dot-dash-dot. "Know what that means? That means *swinehund*. Jerry *swinehund*!"

"Mum, does he have to?" protested Elaine.

"I'm signalling to Jerry!" Dot-dot, dash-dot—

"Look, just *stop* it, will you?"

"But I'm *practising*. I got to be ready for them!" Dot-dash-dot-d—

Elaine gave a short, sharp scream.

"Oh Elaine," said Mum. "Try to be patient."

"But he treats it like a *game*!" Elaine scrunched up her magazine and hurled it viciously across the shelter. "Why can't he just grow up?"

The all clear sounded at long last. They had been in the shelter for hours. Everyone's nerves were frayed, tempers on edge. Mum said that she would put the kettle on.

"But I'm afraid we haven't anything nice to eat. We're right out of biscuits."

"Shall I go and get something?" said Bobbie, hopefully.

"Would you?" said Mum. "Just up to Mrs Beames? That would be kind of you. Jenny, why don't you go with him? Come straight back, mind! I'll have tea waiting."

Jenny and Bobbie walked down the garden path.

"I know why you wanted to come," hissed Jenny. "You just wanted to see what's happened."

"Didn't!"

"Did!"

"Didn't!"

"D—"

Jenny stopped. So did Bobbie. Their hands reached out. They held each other very tightly.

Where Mrs Beames's sweet shop had stood was now a deep hole in the ground.

CHAPTER SEVEN

"Where is Mrs Beames?" faltered Bobbie.

He waited for Jenny to say, "Oh, she'll be all right. She'll have gone in a shelter."

But Jenny didn't. She didn't say anything. She just stood there, frozen, staring at the pit and the pile of rubble.

"Where is she?" Bobbie tugged urgently at his sister's hand.

"I—" Jenny's bottom lip started to tremble.

"She'll have gone in the shelter, won't she? Won't she, Jenny?" Bobbie tugged again, more urgently this time. "*Jennee!* She'll have gone in the shelter!"

Mrs Beames didn't have a shelter of her own but there was a public one on the corner of Styles Road and the High Street. It was only five minutes away. That's where she'd have gone. She'd be safe in the shelter.

"Jenny?" Bobbie's voice came out as a whisper. "Is she in the shelter?"

"You know she won't use them!" cried Jenny.

They wouldn't let cats into public shelters. The

Government had said that cats were best left to roam. "They can look after themselves."

But Mrs Beames wouldn't be parted from Big Tom.

"He's all I've got," she used to say. "Him and my George."

When there was an air raid, Mrs Beames and Big Tom went to sleep on a mattress beneath the kitchen table. But where was the mattress now? Where was the table? Where was the kitchen?

Bobbie swallowed.

"I 'spec' she'll have been rescued," he said. A cosy picture entered his head of Mrs Beames, with Big Tom on her lap, wrapped in a warm blanket at the ARP post, drinking a cup of hot sweet tea. That was what they gave people: hot sweet tea. Mrs Beames would be all right.

He pulled at Jenny's hand. "Let's go and see."

Jenny looked at him. "See what?"

Bobbie was about to say, "See Mrs Beames drinking her tea," but at that moment Mr Gooch, the ARP warden, came running up, shouting and waving his hands.

"Get away, you two! That's a dangerous structure, that is." He pointed at the house next door to Mrs Beames's. "Could cave in any moment. Be off with you!"

"Where is Mrs Beames?" said Bobbie. "Is she drinking tea?"

There was a pause.

"No, lad." Mr Gooch shook his head. "She's not drinking tea."

"Then where is she? If she's not drinking tea… *where is she?*"

Mr Gooch jerked his head at Jenny. "Take him away, there's a good girl."

"Bobbie." Jenny put an arm round Bobbie's shoulders. "We've got to go."

"But what about Mrs Beames? What about Big Tom?"

"We've got to go, Bobbie."

"I don't want to go! I want Big Tom! Where is he?"

Bobbie ran forward. Mr Gooch spread his arms to bar the way, but he wasn't quite quick enough.

"Bobbie, don't look!" screeched Jenny.

She clapped a hand over Bobbie's eyes; but she wasn't quite quick enough either.

"I saw him," wept Bobbie. "I saw him!"

A pathetic scrap of black and white fur. All that was left of Big Tom.

"It's not fair! It isn't fair!" Bobbie broke away from Jenny and began hitting out at a lamppost with his fist. "He was just a cat! He didn't ever hurt anyone!"

"I don't suppose Mrs Beames did either," said Jenny.

"But she was a person! She knew what was happening! Big Tom didn't!"

Jenny felt a sudden flash of anger. Not against the German pilot who had dropped a bomb on top of Mrs Beames, but against her brother. Stupid little boy, thinking war was fun! She felt like screaming at him.

"This is *war*! This is what happens in war!"

But Bobbie's face was twisted with grief, the tears rolling down his cheeks, plopping off on to his collar, and she didn't have the heart.

She said, "Don't cry, Bobbie. They wouldn't have known anything about it."

But what comfort was that? Never again would he buy gobstoppers from Mrs Beames. Never again would he hold Big Tom in his arms and bury his face in his fur.

"Just a poor little cat that never did any harm to anyone!"

"Lots of us have never done any harm to anyone," said Jenny. "But we still have to put up with it."

That evening, down in the Anderson, snug in her armchair, Miss Dunc said that Mrs Beames had "brought it on herself".

"Ridiculous! Not going in the shelter all because of a cat. Now see where it's got her."

It was Elaine who stuck up for Mrs Beames.

"She loved Big Tom! If they'd only let her take him in the shelter with her, they'd both still be alive."

"Oh! Hoity-toity," said Miss Dunc. "And what about all the human beings, pray? If every Tom, Dick and Harry were allowed to take their animals with them, there'd be no room for people."

"Yes, and a good thing too," muttered Elaine. "I can think of some animals I'd sooner have than people."

Miss Dunc paused in the act of removing her teeth. "Would you be referring to anyone in particular?"

Elaine opened her mouth. Mum said, "Elaine!" in warning tones. And that was when Bobbie heard it. A faint mewling sound, from somewhere outside the shelter.

"Quiet!" He jumped to his feet. "*Quiet!*"

They all fell silent, listening.

"I don't hear anything," said Miss Dunc.

Bobbie did. He hurled himself at the door. Mum shrieked, "Bobbie, you come back! Don't you dare to open that door!"

But Bobbie already had. He was out there in the moonlight, with the German bombers somewhere above him, the searchlights sweeping the skies and the anti-aircraft guns blazing. And through it all, the thin miaowing of a cat.

"Big Tom?"

A shape sprang forward out of the vegetable patch. And it was! It was Big Tom! With his whiskers singed and half his tail missing, but still, unmistakably, Tom.

Bobbie swept him into his arms and dived back down again into the shelter.

"Mum, Mum, look!"

"You naughty boy! You could have been killed," scolded Mum. But she didn't sound too angry.

Bobbie sat with Jenny on the camp bed, Big Tom cradled in his arms.

"He must have come looking for you," said Elaine.

Miss Dunc sniffed. "Risking all our lives for a *cat*."

"It's not just a cat," Elaine told her. "It's Big Tom!'

"Poor Tommy." Jenny stroked him under the chin, the way he liked. "Look what's happened to your lovely tail."

Big Tom gave a sad chirrup.

"He must have been so frightened."

"He won't be frightened any more." Bobbie buried his face in Big Tom's fur. "I'll look after you, Tom. Don't worry. You'll be safe with me." He turned to his mum. "The war can't go on much longer, Mum, can it?"

* * *

The war went on until 1945, by which time Bobbie was fifteen and Big Tom about the same. Bobbie kept his word to Big Tom. He looked after him and kept him safe. When Bobbie went into the shelter, so did Tom. Miss Dunc could mutter all she liked. Big Tom was one of the family. He wasn't being left outside!

On VE day, which was Victory in Europe Day, there were celebrations all over Britain. In Scarlet Street, where Bobbie lived, they had a party. Everyone, all up and down the street, joined in. Even Miss Dunc. Tables were set out in the middle of the road, Union Jacks hung from bedroom windows and coloured streamers decorated lampposts. There were crackers and paper hats and even fireworks. Everyone had used up their rations to supply food for the party: sandwiches with spam, or corned beef, or chocolate spread; peanut butter and jellies; rock cakes, carrot cakes and biscuits with jam.

Old Mr Pink at no 45 played the accordion so that people could dance. Jenny, who was now seventeen, danced with her best friend Joan. Mum danced with Dad. Elaine danced with her fiancé, Sam Pringle.

And Derek danced with his girlfriend, Ella. Derek had come home from the war with one of his arms missing, but he could still dance. Oh, he could dance all right! There was nothing wrong with his legs.

There was nothing wrong with Bobbie's legs either. Bobbie ran around excitedly, waving sparklers. Even Miss Dunc got up and did a bit of a twirl with Mr Gooch. Everyone was just so glad that the war was over!

And Bobbie was as glad as anyone.

"Reckon we had just about enough of it," he said to Mr Gooch.

"Reckon we did, young Bobbie," agreed Mr Gooch.

"It was all right at the beginning," said Bobbie. "But it got kind of boring at the end."

"Reckon it did," said Mr Gooch.

Bobbie looked at Big Tom, sitting on the table wearing a paper hat. Big Tom was in his seventh heaven! He was surrounded by *food*.

"You'll be able to go out at night again now," said Bobbie, nodding. "Go out mousing. Be a big real cat."

But the big real cat had just hooked a slice of spam off someone's plate when they weren't looking.

Never mind mousing! Big Tom licked his paw and rubbed it over his whiskers.

This was the life!

Order Form

To order direct from the publishers, just make a list of the titles you want and fill in the form below:

Name ....

Address ....

....

....

Send to: Dept 6, HarperCollins Publishers Ltd, Westerhill Road, Bishopbriggs, Glasgow G64 2QT.

Please enclose a cheque or postal order to the value of the cover price, plus:

UK & BFPO: Add £1.00 for the first book, and 25p per copy for each additional book ordered.

Overseas and Eire: Add £2.95 service charge. Books will be sent by surface mail but quotes for airmail despatch will be given on request.

A 24-hour telephone ordering service is available to holders of Visa, MasterCard, Amex or Switch cards on 0141- 772 2281.

Collins
An *Imprint* of HarperCollins*Publishers*